MAC A. RONI VISITS THE SUPERMARKET

This book is dedicated to my husband, Brad, who unfailingly supports me in all my dreams; my sons, Jaxon and Braylon, for making me smile and see God's love every day; my mom, Renae, who encouraged my imagination; my dad, Dwight, who taught me the value of hard work; and my sister, Katie, who gave me all the "literature genes"

Use Your Noodle!

MAC A. RONI VISITS THE SUPERMARKET

Written by Jessica Braithwait
Illustrated by Dian Wang

Edited by Jenny Bowman

Printed by CreateSpace, An Amazon.com Company
Available from Amazon.com and other retail outlets

ISBN-13: 978-0692792377 (Jessica Braithwait)
ISBN-10: 0692792376

Your children can discover more fantastically fun enrichment activities with Mac and his friends at www.useyournoodlemac.com

Readers will "use their noodles" while practicing the following objectives:

1. Count objects using one-to-one correspondence.
2. Use "more" and "less" comparison vocabulary.
3. Compare attributes of items with "heavier" and "lighter" vocabulary.
4. Identify the scale as a measurement for weight.
5. Count backward starting at ten.
6. Identify shapes such as circles, rectangles, squares and triangles.
7. Identify ordinal positions first through fourth.
8. Practice simple addition up to five.

This is Mac A. Roni,
But you can call him Mac!
He loves taking adventures with friends,
To keep his brain on track!

Math helps him solve problems every day,
Whether it be at the park, pool, or grocery store.
Without wonderful math in our world,
Our days would be such a bore!

We can use our noodles,
To think really hard,
To help Mac solve problems,
In school or our own backyard!

Mac loved math. He liked counting and numbers and finding sums. Mac and his mother are going to the supermarket today to pick up some healthy afternoon snacks and sides for dinner. The first thing Mac noticed when he walked into the store were the brown baskets full of delicious green and red apples!

SALE

¥ 3.⁵⁰

SALE

¥ 3.²⁰

"May we please buy some apples?" asked Mac.

"Of course dear," said Mac's mother. "But first let's put your brain to the test and do some math. Which basket has more apples in it?"

Mac liked counting. First he studied the baskets and then pointed to each red apple as he said a number.

Next, Mac counted the green apples. He pointed to each green apple as he said a number. "Since there are nine red apples and six green apples, there are MORE red apples than green apples!" said Mac.

"That is correct Mac!" exclaimed Mac's mother. "Way to use your noodle! Now let's go get some ears of corn for dinner tonight!"

"I want you to get
ten ears of corn for me
from the bin, but when you
put them into the cart, you need to
count them backwards!" said Mac's mother.

Mac was excited about this math challenge. He found the corn and counted. Since he was counting backwards this time, he started at number ten! Each time he said a number, he put another ear of corn into the cart.

"Excellent work! Way to use your noodle,"
said Mac's mother.
"Let's go get some nuts to make trail mix."

As Mac and his mother approached the barrels of mixed nuts, Mac noticed a funny silver basket sitting on a clock.

"Mom, what is that funny clock thing? Do nuts need to tell time?" asked Mac.

"That is not a clock Mac," laughed Mac's mother. "That is a scale. A scale is used to measure how much things weigh. I want two pounds of cashews. Scoop the cashews onto the scale until the scale reads two pounds."

Mac scooped the cashews onto the scale until the scale's red arm pointed to two pounds.

"Amazing work!" proclaimed Mac's mother. "Now I need four pounds of almonds."
Mac scooped almonds onto the scale until the red arm pointed to the number four.

"Fantastic," said Mac's mother, "but I have a question that will make you use your noodle! Which bag is LIGHTER?"
Mac thought hard about this math question.

"Since the almonds weigh four pounds and the cashews weigh two pounds, the CASHEWS are lighter!" said Mac.
"Correct again!" said Mac's mother proudly.

Mac and his mother continued on their supermarket journey. As they turned to walk down the next aisle, Mac's mother was stunned with how many shapes she saw!

"Mac! Look at all these wonderful shapes surrounding us! I see triangles, squares, rectangles, and circles!" exclaimed Mac's mother. Mac looked around. "Really?" said Mac. "I don't see many shapes at all!"

"Oh Mac," said Mac's mother. "Use your noodle! Shapes are all around us, and if you look, you can find some. Try to point some shapes out to me!"

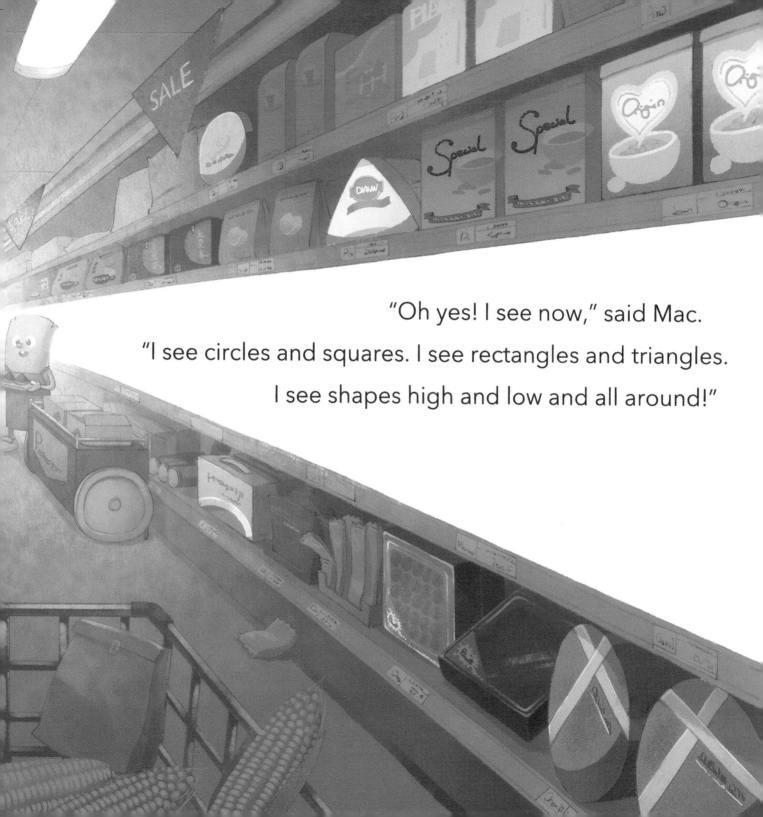

"Oh yes! I see now," said Mac.
"I see circles and squares. I see rectangles and triangles.
I see shapes high and low and all around!"

"Fantastic shape discoveries Mac!" said Mac's mother as she
put a few boxes of crackers into her cart. "I believe we are
ready to check out!"

Mac and his mother pulled their cart up to checkout counter fifteen. The line was long! It was a very busy day at the supermarket!

"Are we first in line Mac?" asked Mac's mother.

"I don't think so," said Mac. "There are too many people in front of us for us to be first in line."

"You are right. We are not first in line. What position in line are we?" asked Mac's mother.

"Well, my best friend Beau is at the front, so he is FIRST. Cheerleader Lynn Guini is SECOND and Farmer Manny Cotti is THIRD. We are behind Manny, so that puts us in the FOURTH position!"

"Brilliant!" said Mac's mother. She was beaming with pride.

When Mac and his
mother reached the front
of the line, he placed three ears of
corn and two apples on the conveyor belt.
"It's time to use your noodle again," said Mac's mother.
"How many items are there on the belt altogether?"

"Hmmm," thought Mac. "To find out how many there are in all, I need to count the ears of corn AND the apples........ FIVE! Three plus two more is five!"

As Mac and his mother left the supermarket, Mac smiled thinking about how many times he had to use his noodle! He loved doing math and was excited for his next math adventure!

About the Author

Jessica is a mom, wife, former teacher, and current photographer from Nebraska. She graduated from the University of Nebraska Kearney with degrees in special education and elementary education. Mac A. Roni's adventures have lived in her dreams since she was fifteen years old. She enjoys spending time and laughing with her husband, Brad, and two sons, Jaxon and Braylon.

About the Illustrator

Dian Wang is an illustrator focusing on children's books & APP. She works from her home illustration studio in Changsha, a beautiful mid city in China, where she's living with her husband, son, and cat.

59504063R00020

Made in the USA
Lexington, KY
07 January 2017